There is no color on the tundra in winter, no color and no sound except the howling of winds and wolves.

Arctic Fox wears his winter white coat. No one can see him, he blends so perfectly into the miles and miles of snow.

But the boy and his mama see the tracks on the snowy path around their cabin. They smile.

It is good to know they are not alone.

Circle of

BY SUSI GREGG FOWLER

ILLUSTRATED BY PETER CATALANOTTO

SCHOLASTIC INC.

New York   Toronto   London   Auckland   Sydney
Mexico City   New Delhi   Hong Kong   Buenos Aires

Spring finally comes. Grasses poke through the wet snow and shiver in the cool air. The heavy rains turn white to brown. The ground is squishy and wet as the boy and his mama hurry to the river. *Slurp, slurp*, go the boy's boots as the wet tundra tries to suck them in.

River Otter's pups are sure to be out of the den. Hers are the first youngsters every spring, and the boy is eager to greet the newcomers.

"Hello, pup," he says to a small brown creature sliding alone on the riverbank. "Where's your mother?"

Mother Otter is probably in her nearby den.

"She'll be back soon," Mama says. After all, Otter Pup doesn't know how to swim yet.

Suddenly there is a splash. Otter Pup tumbles into deep water and she cannot get out. Mama hesitates only a moment. Then she strides into the icy river, grabs Otter Pup like a wet kitten, and deposits her on the bank.

"There, now. You wait for your mother before you go swimming again."

Otter Pup blinks, then turns and runs toward home.

She doesn't say thank you, but Mama doesn't mind. What can you expect from an otter pup?

In just a few weeks, the tundra changes completely. Color skips across the land. Green clumps of willows and berry bushes and bright patches of buttercups and marsh marigolds are everywhere. Swans, geese, and sandhill cranes nest in the wet grasses.

Otter Pup is a skilled swimmer now and a good fisher, too. One day she climbs up the riverbank, dragging a grayling. Raven watches closely from behind some willow brush. For once he is silent. His wing is injured and he doesn't want his enemies to see him.

Raven holds perfectly still, but he cannot hide from Otter Pup. She spots him and his injured wing. Raven looks with longing at Otter Pup's fish.

Suddenly, Otter Pup drops her fish. Raven hops forward and snatches it, never taking his eyes off Otter Pup. He hides behind the willows again and gobbles up the fish before anyone can take it from him.

He doesn't say thank you, but Otter Pup doesn't mind. What can you expect from a raven?

In time, Raven heals. He flies again over the tundra, snatching berries, stealing fish from other animals, and making noise wherever he goes.

One morning, Raven sees something near a clump of dwarf birch and swoops down for a better look. It's a lost caribou calf, separated from her mother. Looks like the wolves will get this one. Raven sits on a branch and watches the long-legged creature. Caribou Calf stares back with giant, frightened eyes.

"*Cr-r-ruck!*" Raven squawks, then squawks again. Other ravens respond to his scratchy call. They hover above Caribou Calf like a noisy black cloud. Mother Caribou notices the gathering of ravens and comes pounding over the tundra. Together again, Caribou Calf and her mother glance up at Raven circling above them.

They don't say thank you, but Raven doesn't mind. What can you expect from caribou?

Mother Caribou and her calf rejoin the herd, heading toward the coast to escape the mosquitoes and flies. The sun never goes down. It is high summer, the time of light.

And then change comes again. The sun sets for the first time in weeks. Autumn is not far off. Some of the waterfowl begin their migration south. The caribou, too, are on the move again.

Mother Caribou hears a whimper. She heads toward the sound, leaving the herd. It is an arctic fox, caught in a trap. He is a sad sight, scruffy and exhausted from trying to escape. His mottled fur is still changing from summer brown to white. When he sees Mother Caribou, Arctic Fox is afraid. Caribou's big hooves and strong legs could make short work of him.

Mother Caribou's hoof lands on the steel trap and springs it open. Then she silently moves on. Arctic Fox is free. He moves away as quickly as his injured paw allows.

He doesn't say thank you, but Mother Caribou doesn't mind. What can you expect from an arctic fox?

Day after day, Arctic Fox nurses his paw until it is healed. His coat is
completely white again.

Winter is almost here. The boy has been watching the sky. Mama
tells him the snow will come soon. If he wants enough berries to last
until spring, he'd better go picking one final time.

There aren't many berries left, and it takes a long time to fill both
buckets. The boy's hands are cold, and he is glad to finish up and put
his mittens back on. He'd better hurry home for supper.

As the boy turns to go, his ankle twists under him. "Ouch!" he cries and tumbles down. His precious berries scatter. He crawls around, picking up all he can. When he tries to stand, he collapses. He cannot walk.

"Mama!" the boy calls, but Mama cannot hear him. He begins to crawl toward home. The light is disappearing quickly, and the bitter cold stings his cheeks.

Soft as feathers, snow begins to fall. The boy takes a deep breath and crawls some more. He stops and takes off a mitten in order to eat a few berries. Then he gasps. He can just make out Arctic Fox in the deepening twilight.

Would an arctic fox hurt a boy alone in the dark?

Suddenly Arctic Fox darts forward and grabs his mitten.

"Come back, thief!" cries the boy. But Arctic Fox doesn't come back.

At home, Mama wonders where the boy is.
He knows better than to be late for supper.
The darkness and the weather worry her.
She'd better look for him.

Mama steps outside. His mitten! "Where are you?" she calls, but no one is there. Then where did the mitten come from?

Mama shines a light into the darkness. Tracks in the fallen snow lead up to the mitten and disappear behind the woodpile. They are the tracks of Arctic Fox. Mama cannot see where the tracks begin. Perhaps if she follows them, she will find her boy.

The wind begins to blow, and the snow is falling faster. If Mama doesn't hurry, the snow will cover the delicate prints.

Mama never notices Arctic Fox, gliding like a shadow in the falling snow. But he trails behind her, silent and unseen. Not until Mama finds the boy and lifts him into her arms does Arctic Fox disappear into the night.

On the way home, Mama tells the boy about the appearance of his mitten and the tracks that led her to him. The boy remembers Arctic Fox.

"Thank you," he whispers into the night air.

His words are carried on the wind.

They float past Arctic Fox as he hurries home.

They circle around Mother Caribou, asleep with her calf.

They sail over Raven, hunched on a bare willow branch.

They slip into a den in the frozen river and whisper to Otter Pup.

And they come back to where they began — back to the boy
and back to his mama, back to the cabin all cozy and warm.
The boy and his mama smile at each other.

It is good to know they are not alone.

To Janice Gregg Levy and Walter Gregg —
my sister and brother, my companions and friends. *S. G. F.*

For Maddy and Nina   *P. C.*

No part of this work may be reproduced in whole or in part, or stored in a retrieval system, or transmitted in any form or by any means, electronic, mechanical, photocopying, recording, or otherwise, without written permission of the publisher. For information regarding permission, write to Scholastic Inc., Attention: Permissions Department, 555 Broadway, New York, NY 10012.

12 11 10 9 8 7 6 5 4 3 2   3 4 5 / 0

Printed in the U.S.A.   08

ISBN 0-590-10069-6

First Scholastic paperback printing, October 2001

Hand lettering by Anthony Bloch
The text type was set in Cooper Old Style.
The illustrations in this book were painted in watercolor.
Book design by Marijka Kostiw